DARKMIST

A Luminescence Novella
BOOK 4

J.L. WEIL

A LUMINESCENCE NOVELLA

NOVELLA

BOOK FOUR

Chapter One

Thumbing through the pages of my astronomy textbook, I lifted my head. Only nine minutes had passed since I sat down, and all I could think was, *why the hell had I taken astronomy?*

Maybe because the idea of taking a biology class made me want to hurl. I mean, I had to dissect a frog in high school. God only knew what they were going to make me dismember in college. Gross. Ick. That's why I was sitting in room 103 of the Natural Science building at the University of North Carolina.

The ten-minute hike across campus was convenient, as was living in the dorms, especially since I was a stickler for time management. No way was I getting stuck sitting in the front row.

Wouldn't it be easier to live here at home? Aunt Clara's voice filtered into my thoughts.

Accessibility hadn't been the only reason I'd chosen to stay in the dorms. I'd wanted the full college experience, a fragment of freedom to discover myself. It had taken a bit of convincing for Aunt Clara to agree to the co-ed dorms, particularly because my edible boyfriend's room was down the hall.

Gavin Mason.

He was not the kind of guy I ever pictured myself dating. Dark. Mysterious. Edgy. Dimples that made his blue eyes twinkle devilishly. And he was a witch...like me.

I still wasn't sure what he saw in me, but living under the same roof definitely had its perks. Gavin had taken a slightly different approach to college than I had. Where I was laser focused on my studies, he was motivated by the next party.

Austin and Gavin had become frat brothers in the sense they'd found a shared love of Alpha Beta Delta or whatever weird Greek name their fraternity. It was kind of a surprise. I never would have pegged my boyfriend as a frat boy. He was more of a loner. And that made me think he was up to something. He always had an agenda.

The question was, what?

I extended my legs under the seat in front of mine and glanced at the clock above the door. Ugh. If this was how my day was going to go, then I was in trouble. My eyes wandered about the classroom, checking out the other dorks that were dumb enough to sign up for this course.

There was a girl with cinnamon and spice hair a few seats diagonal from where I was. It wasn't her fiery hair that captured my wandering gaze, but what she was doing with her pen. The two of us should have been taking notes on the lecture Professor Burns so snoringly delivered, yet...

I had no excuse, but this girl, she was concentrating intently on the slim silver pen hovering in the air an inch or two from her face. Nothing was touching it. No fingers. No string. No trick. Except magic.

I felt the tremble of power dance in the air, and she suddenly had my undivided attention. *WTF.* She was openly using magic in the middle of class. I was flabbergasted. My mouth fell open. Did she have no regard for the safeguard of the craft?

I mean, I was still an apprentice in a manner of speaking, but even as a novice, I knew the rules. There was no doubt, this girl was a witch, but the difference between us was, I didn't flaunt my gifts. I didn't openly splash magic where others could see.

But as my eyes swept over the room, I realized no one else noticed anything amiss. *A cloaking charm?* It was the only explanation my mind could come up with. *I* could see through the spell, given the extent of my powers.

There was nothing ordinary about the magic I was born with. Nothing at all. My power was feared by most witches and coveted by the darker ones. I'd learned to accept who I was—the descendant of Morgana Le Fey—a clàr silte.

It wasn't as cool as it sounded.

The CliffNotes version was, I sucked the magic from other witches. I was the Dementor of enchantresses. Of course, there were repercussions for such power. I couldn't just go around slurping magic from every witch I encountered like they were ninety-nine cent cherry Slurpee's. The price for using magic of that magnitude left blemishes on my soul—the sort of marks that turned your soul dark.

And I'd rather punt-kick myself in the face than losing myself to dark magic. I didn't like who I turned into, or the little voices in my head, baiting me to take more. One taste led to an insatiable appetite.

To date, I'd only stripped one witch of his power. Lukas Devine. I hadn't seen or heard from him since that day. It was probably for the best. Lukas had nefarious plans where I was concerned. It was still hard to believe I'd mistaken his feelings toward me as affection, when in fact he wanted my power and what I could do with it.

Gavin, if given the chance, would love to go a round or two with Lukas, to screw up his pretty boy face, as he would say. I shuddered at the thought of them running into each other. Bloodbath.

As I stared the redheaded witch, she must have sensed my eyes on her. Her head angled, meeting my disapproving gaze dead on, but she never dropped the spell. Actually, the minx smiled at me, and not in a friendly sort of way. It was menacing and made my skin prickle with unease. There was something off about her.

I tapped my pencil on the blank paper in front of me and bit my lip.

She lifted her brow when I continued to stare. It was a challenge. The pen floating parallel to her slender nose began to spin. Then with a flick of her marshmallow painted fingernail, she sent the pen sailing through the air, directly at Professor Burns.

I froze.

The length of the pen whizzed past his ear and

the tip sunk into the corkboard bulletin behind him with a *thump*. I made a loud audible gasped.

Holy shitsnacks.

Professor Burns brushed at the side of his head, but other than that, he didn't miss a beat in his lecture. However, my disruptive gasp of horror was a different story. Numerous heads turned my way, giving me the side-eye reserved for public spectacles.

My face flamed an ugly shade of pink. Dipping down, I let my hair fall forward, curtaining my face as my gripped tightened on my pencil. If there was one thing I hated more than being embarrassed, it was bullies. Silently, cursing a string of swear words that would have made my aunt blush, I peeked up from under my lashes.

The *witch* was laughing at me.

Swirls of magic gathered at my fingertips. I wanted to show this witch what real magic was. These parlor tricks were high school compared to what I could do.

But noooo. That's not why I was here, I reminded myself. Sometimes it just plain sucked being the good girl.

For the remaining of class, I avoided looking at her. I didn't want to play her games.

As soon as Professor Burns dismissed the class, I

shot out of my seat like I was racing for the last cup of coffee. I made it to the double doors without tripping or mowing anyone down. Bursting out of the science building, I lifted my head up and breathed in the warm afternoon sun. There was a hint of sea in the air, but I didn't stop to smell the roses. My legs kept moving. I wanted to put as much distance as I could between the mysterious witch and me. She struck a chord inside me. And not in a good way.

"You're a witch," a dark seductive voice stated.

I stopped in my tracks. The multi-hued ginger was sitting on a bench just outside the brick library, twirling a piece of her hair.

How the hell had she gotten here before me? The library was adjacent to my dorm, a win-win in my book. "I don't know what you're talking about," I replied. This girl was a stranger to me, and I surely didn't owe her an explanation.

"You saw me in there. I know you did." She crossed her legs over an expensive pair of designer jeans. "I can feel your power, you know. It's pointless to lie."

Most witches could sense another of their kind. "I saw you showing off with a juvenile spell."

The smirk on her lips tightened. "I'd be careful who you piss off, rookie."

"I'm not looking for trouble," I said, before I said something she'd regret.

Her cherry lips puckered. "That's too bad. Trouble is way more fun. I'm Amara, by the way."

"Brianna," I replied, shifting the strap of my bag higher up on my shoulder.

She batted her heavily mascara-framed cat green eyes and stood up, pulling a slim card out from her back pocket. "Here. If you're interested, there's a party tonight at my sorority house. It's not your typical sorority, and I think you'd fit right in. I'm the house advisor."

I took the business card, but I doubted this *so-called sorority*, was approved by the school board, or if it was, a dab of magic had been involved. Last I checked there wasn't a major for witchcraft. "I'll pass," I answered, trying to keep the distain from my voice. "I have a full load this semester and hadn't really thought about rushing."

She shrugged. "Suit yourself. If you change your mind, you know where to find me, Brianna. My number's on the card." Twitching her butt, she turned back toward me after only a step or two. She popped a pair of shades over her eyes. "Hope to see you tonight."

A cold chill passed over me as I watched her saunter down the sidewalk like she was on the red carpet.

Geez.

I flipped the card over in my hand. Kappa Zeta Gamma. *If you can't fly with the big girls, get off the broom.*

Catchy. And not too subtle.

Under the tagline was her name. Amara Sanders. There was also the sorority logo. KZG. And no joke, there was a little wooden broom going through the monogram.

Wow. And to think I thought I wasn't going to make any friends. I hadn't thought I would meet a witch, or that I would accuse of her misusing magic. What a way to make a first impression. New city. New school. And I managed to muck it up in less than thirty minutes. Could be a personal record.

Chapter Two

Dropping my enormous astronomy book on my desk, I flopped on my dorm bed, staring at the twinkle lights dangling across the ceiling. My roommate was an interior decorator major who was obsessed with Pinterest.

Kylie was a petite brunette with skin that was golden year round and a sparkling personality. Her wardrobe reflected her flare for design, and would have made Tori green with envy.

It was strange not having Tori here, but university wasn't for her. She was furthering her education at Elite School of Beauty. I didn't doubt I was going to end up being her guinea pig on her journey to become a beautician. I only hoped that I would have hair left by the time she graduated. My only comfort was that any damage she caused could be fixed with a little bit of magic.

I missed her, especially after today.

Twirling the card between my fingers, I did something I never thought I would do. I considered joining a sorority, or the very least, checking out the house. The way I saw it, I had two choices: I could go to this party tonight and maybe meet a few cool people, or I could climb into bed, turn off all the lights, and pull the covers over my head. I so wanted to indulge myself in a good pity party, but my curiosity got the best of me. I hadn't busted my butt working all those summers at Mystic Floral, saving money for college, and taking on the additional expense of living on campus, just so I could shut myself up in my room. *The whole experience, remember.* And that included parties.

I nibbled on my nail, contemplating.

Forget it.

If I had to think this hard, it wasn't worth it. Maybe meeting other witches wasn't a good idea. Who knows what might happen. Honestly, I had better things to do with my time than get wasted with a bunch of uppity sorority sisters.

Like writing a paper for Composition I.

Unwilling to give Amara and her sorority another thought, I pulled out my English textbook. My classes were finished for the day, but my run-in with Amara had interrupted my plans. I had intended to head over to the financial building after my astronomy class to fill out an application for a campus job. At eighteen credit hours, I had a full schedule, but if I was going to continue living on campus, I was going to need to money, and a job on campus seemed like the best route.

I was going to have to make time tomorrow.

Tonight, I was going to attack my homework with a vengeance. And I did for a few hours, before I felt the fireflies flutter in my belly. There was only one person who enticed those warm flurries. Gavin. A rush of excitement whirled inside me.

My eyes lifted. He was leaning in the doorway, his startling blue eyes were vibrant and alive, a stark contrast against his midnight hair. The cool metal hoop at the center of his lip twitched as they curved. Gavin was gorgeous in a way that made me feel giddy and reckless.

Climbing off the bed, I jumped into his arms and buried my face into the alcove between his shoulder and neck. I inhaled the light scent of his cologne. Bedazzling. He smelled good and safe. A head taller than me, his strong arms wrapped around my waist, keeping me close.

"I'm glad to see you, too," he murmured into my hair.

I pulled back so I could look into his eyes. Unable to help myself, I pressed my lips to his. My fingers weaved into his silky hair. It still surprised me that even though I saw him daily, my heart yearned for him. "I missed you," I whispered against his lips, his hoop scraping lightly over my mouth.

He brushed away a strand of hair that had drifted into my face. "If I'd known you were going to attack me, I would have come by much sooner."

I grinned, rolling my eyes. "Are you going somewhere?" I asked. He was dressed in distressed jeans and a dark shirt, his hair intentional styled to look as if he just gotten out of bed.

"We are," he replied. "Get dressed." Then he proceeded to give me a swat on the butt.

I squeaked. "I am dressed."

He flashed me a grin. "As much as I love you in your Harley Quinn mile-high socks and little red shorts, I'd rather not get into a fight tonight."

"They're knee-high socks," I argued, wiggling my toes, although I was impressed he knew who Harley Quinn was. But he was right. I couldn't actually go out wearing this. I'd been so busy studying that I had forgotten what I looked like.

"And where is it you think you're dragging me to?"

"A party, and before you argue, I am not letting you spend your Friday night alone in your room."

Flopping back down on my bed, I frowned. "I can't go out tonight. I have an assignment to finish for English and a quiz to study for." I'd already turned down one party.

He pushed my textbook aside and sat down next to me. "You work too hard, always pushing yourself. If you don't take a breath and have a little fun, your entire college experience will have passed you by."

Okay, I didn't know what he had up his sleeve, but as much as I needed to lighten up, there was something fishy going on. My brows knitted together. "Why do you really want to go to this party? I'm not buying that you've suddenly turned into a frat douche."

An amused expression settled on his striking face. "Fine. I actually hate frat parties, but there is supposedly a coven of witches on campus. I want to check them out. See if they're going to be a problem."

The words *problem* and *witches* in the same sentence had my internal alarm picking up. My thoughts automatically turned to Amara. "Where did you hear this tip?"

He shrugged. "Jared."

Oh wow. That's a reliable source. Except this time, Gavin's brother might be onto something. I tapped my finger on my leg. "Fine, give me five minutes to change."

Not entirely enthusiastic about my evening plans, I started rummaging around my room, looking for something clean to wear. Laundry was not any more fun to do in college. I found a semi-clean pair of jeans and started to shimmy out of my shorts. Then I remembered Gavin was still in the room. "What are you doing?"

He was kicked back on my bed, an arm propped behind his head. "I like watching you get dressed."

I rolled my eyes, tugging the pair of jeans over my hips. "I bet you do. Should I get you some popcorn for the show?"

He chuckled as I managed to squeeze my butt into the jeans and loop the button. "What's this?" he asked.

I turned my head to the side to see him holding the card Amara had given me between his fingers. "You're not the only one who got invited to a party," I grumbled.

He lips turned down. "Why didn't you tell me?"

I shrugged. "Because I had no intention of going."

His eyes ran over the card. "Who gave you this?"

"A girl in my astronomy class. What makes you think there is something corrupt about these witches?" I asked.

Watching me with a crocked smile on his lips, his gaze roamed lazily over my body. "Just a girl...or a witch?"

If he kept looking at me like that, we were never going to make it to this party. As much as I would rather stay home with Gavin and his blessed lips, my curiosity was peaked. "Why do I get the feeling you already know the answer?"

Shift to his side, he slipped his hand into his back pocket and pulled out a little card identical in size as mine. "Because I got one as well."

My eyes narrowed. "Well, isn't that dandy?"

All of sudden, Gavin was sitting upright on the bed, his eyes sharpening. "What happened?"

"Why must something have happened?"

"You hate parties, and you're biting your lip."

"That's not true," I replied, and then dragged my bottom lip into my mouth with my front teeth. As soon as I realized what I was doing, I stopped.

He arched a brow, the twinkling lights overhead catching the glint of silver from the stud. My boyfriend had more piercings than I did.

Sighing, I found the top I'd been searching for under a stack of notebooks. "Okay. I met this girl in class today. She's a witch." I snatched the purple crop top out from under the pile heavy enough to throw my arm out.

"And..." he prompted.

I grabbed the ends of my tank and tugged it over my head. "I don't know. She gave me bad mojo." I yanked on the shirt and shook my hair out.

He looked disappointed. "Why didn't you say anything?"

I took a seat in my desk chair, sliding my feet into a pair of flip-flops. "I was going to, but I saw you standing in my doorway and it slipped my mind. Then you started ordering me about."

Lips curved, he swung his legs over the bed. "That's hilarious. As if you ever do anything I ask." He looped a finger into the waistband of my jeans and tugged me forward so I was in between his legs.

My fingers entwined through his hair. "I do if you ask nicely." I leaned down, staring at his lips and...

Austin's voice carried through the hall and into my room. "Hey, babygirl, where you at?"

Gavin pressed his forehead into my belly, and sighed. "I forgot. I invited Austin."

"You didn't," I grumbled.

My best friend from high school poked around the door. His brown hair was slicked back and his bottle green eyes were bright with excitement. "Get your hot ass out here. We got witches to hunt."

I took a step back and glanced at Gavin, my lips turned down. "If anything happens to him, I'm holding you responsible. I can't believe you told him."

He winced. "What could possibly happen with us by his side?" Gavin and Austin were roomies. And knowing Austin, he viewed this party as a game, like Clue.

I lifted my brows. Gavin and I both knew the kind of shenanigans I could get into.

Getting my friends mixed up with this part of my life was still hard to accept. I wanted to protect them. I knew all magic wasn't bad, but my experience was limited. All I had to go on was what I'd seen.

Chapter Three

The university campus was beautiful and historic. Trees lined the walkways. White pillars decorated the entrances. Fresh, clean air, the ocean breeze, and everything you needed was in walking distance. There was a peacefulness about the place, with the warm glow of lights illuminating the dormitories.

Our dorm was on the west side of campus, Cornerstone Hall. Hiking it to the other side of the postcard-worthy grounds, we entered what was known as sorority row. Instead of the apartment-like structures freshmen lived in, here quad houses sat side by side. Each had a covered porch full of college students. The chatter of laughter and fun carried over the road. A couple of guys were tossing around a football in the yard. Half-empty bottles of beer were scattered on the stoop and porch ledge.

Shoving my hands into my back pockets, I walked up the stairs and into the house, Gavin and Austin flanking me on either side.

Holy crap.

The house was jam-packed. There was a mean game of beer pong going on in the side room. Music pumped through the house, the bass rumbling under my feet. People were everywhere: crowding the kitchen, lounging on the couch, hanging out in the garage.

Austin's eyes scanned the room. "So what are we looking for? Pointy shoes? Black hats? Warts?"

I jabbed him in the gut. "Have you ever seen me with anyone of those things?"

"Uh, there was the one time in ninth grade. You had this thing growing on—"

"Do you want me to turn you into a toad?" I threatened in a level tone.

He shot me a shit-eating grin. "I was kidding. You look all uptight. Relax, ho." He squeezed my hand.

Easier said than done. I was uptight by nature.

"Try to have fun," Gavin said. "And whatever you do, don't set anything on fire. I'm going to get us drinks."

Frowning, Gavin meandered his way through the crowd toward the back of the house. *Maybe this wasn't such a good idea.* Call it intuition or a premonition, but I couldn't shake the feeling something was going to happen. I squeezed passed a girl who could barely stand up as Austin pulled me across the room.

He dropped an arm over my shoulder. "Let's own this party."

I let a nervous giggle. *He was joking, right?*

There was a high-pitched squeal behind us, and I turned around and came face to face with Amara. She had a grin plastered on her heart-shaped face. "I was beginning to give up on you," she said, acting like we were BFFs. The dress she wore made me want to cover my eyes.

I had the shittiest luck known to man.

She wasn't alone. There were two other girls with her, one on either side of her. Witches. The glimmer of magic shimmered in the air around the three of them, and if I had the ability to see auras, theirs would radiate as only a witch's could.

The one on Amara's right had ultra-shiny black hair in a pixie cut. She was tall and slender, with a meekness in her soft smile. She didn't look like a girl who would be friends with someone like Amara, with her dominating personality.

The other wasn't rail thin or looking like she was dying for a box of Krispy Kremes, but the few extra pounds looked good on her. She had a pretty face, framed by straight, caramel-colored hair with blonde highlights.

I assumed they were sorority sisters.

I gave Amara a bland look. "You're not the only one surprised," I remarked.

"Hmm. I didn't take you as a party girl," she said, flipping her ponytail off her shoulder.

By the end of the night, I had a feeling I would be ready to chop her crimson ponytail off. She rubbed me the wrong way, and I immediately regretted coming. "I'm not."

"Yet, here you are. Does this mean you're reconsidering my offer to join my sorority?"

Austin cleared his throat. "Bri? In a sorority?" He proceeded to laugh. Loudly.

"A friend of yours?" Amara asked, her eyes sliding to Austin.

I was torn between wanting to smack him on the back of the head or rush him to the dorm and tuck him safely in bed. I didn't want to introduce him to Amara. "Austin, this is Amara. We have Astronomy together."

"It's such a blow-off class," she said. The two

girls at her side giggled. "Willow and Ophelia, this is Brianna, the KZG's newest member, as soon as we convince her to rush next week."

The mere thought of rush week made me scrunch my nose in a not-so-pretty way.

Austin opened his mouth, but I conveniently stepped on his foot. He frowned. The last thing I wanted was for him to slip up and tell Amara more than I wanted her to know. Some things were better left a secret.

My powers were one of them.

"Like I said before, I appreciate the offer, but I just don't have time for any...extra activities," I answered.

Amara wasn't deterred. "I'll wear you down, eventually."

Austin leaned in and muttered from the corner of his mouth, "What is she talking about?"

"It's not important," I mumbled.

Amara and her two minions turned to whisper among themselves. Something or someone had caught their attention. I searched the room for Gavin, wondering why he hadn't returned with our drinks.

"Six o'clock, ladies. Check the dimples on that one," I heard Amara purr. "Hmm, and he's headed this way."

Ophelia, who I thought was the rounder one, sucked in a breath as she zeroed in on their target. "Ooooh. He's scrumptious, all yummy and bad."

Amara pursed her red-hot lips. "And if my radar is on point, he's not your typical frat boy. It's about damn time this school gets a guy with a bit more spark."

The three of them giggled.

Amara leaned forward so her hip was popped out, emphasizing her model curves. It was natural to be jealous of someone who looked like Amara. Flawless. Her confidence only added to her sexiness. "Watch me work my magic, girls." Then she giggled at her own poorly said pun. With a flirtatious swagger I'd never have, Amara walked in front of me, strutting her stuff.

I frowned.

Austin's eyes widened, and he snickered under his breath.

I dragged my gaze from Austin and looked to see what poor sap she planned to make her next victim. Amara didn't strike me as the type of her girl who took relationships seriously. Deep in my gut, I already knew who the target was. It was Gavin. As far as I could tell, he was the only guy here with magical abilities.

I saw him in the sea of people walking toward

me. He was utterly clueless about what was about to cross his path. With two bottles in one and a red solo cup in the other, his eyes collided with mine. He lifted a brow at my scowling face, but my gaze flickered over him and zeroed back on Amara. Crossing my arms, I shot her a look that was all kinds of dirty.

"Whoa, he's even better up close," Willow giggled.

My head snapped in her direction. "He's my boyfriend."

Willow and Ophelia had twin looks of shock. "Awkward," they sang in unison.

My heart did a series of acrobatics as Amara's hand touched Gavin's arm. The simple action sent me into a tizzy. Magic roared to my fingertips. "I'm going to zap her to Pluto," I muttered.

"Oh shit, Bri," Austin said, seeing my eyes start to glow violet. "Take a chill pill."

I watched her press her chest right up against him and smile seductively. Thunder roared in my ears. My gaze honed in on one redheaded witch with a death wish. "That witch," I seethed.

Austin shook his head. "Oh no—"

But it was too late. Whatever else he said was lost on me, because I was pushing my way through the crowd. Anger rolled off me in waves. Who did this girl think she was? In the distance, thunder cracked and the sky lit up, beaming through the windows. *That...that tramp.*

Gavin's eyes sought out mine. If a storm was coming, he knew nine out of ten times it was my fault. "What's going on?" he asked, handing me the red cup.

I didn't care what was in, taking a long swig.

Austin rubbed the back of his neck, sensing the sudden rise in tension. He clung onto the neck of the glass bottle. I hadn't realized he was right behind me. "Drama," he serenaded.

"Nothing," I said dryly, taking another gulp of my drink, eyes stuck on Amara.

Her red-painted lips twisted into a sneer. "Are you guys related?"

Bitch please.

Gavin was looking at me with concern when he answered. "She's my girlfriend."

My chin tipped.

She batted her long, lush lashes. "Huh. You don't look like his type."

Oh, and Amara was? That was it.

Austin said my name again, but I was beyond hearing. My face felt like it was on fire. I didn't even remember throwing my drink in her face. One minute I was shooting daggers at her, the next

Amara was dripping wet and covered in rum and coke. Chunks of ice fell at her feet.

There was a uniform gasp that rang from the surrounding group. Gavin's lips twitched. Austin's hand flew to his mouth as he barely restrained bouts of laughter.

In a shriek that could shatter glass, Amara leaped. From the look of pure outrage on her face, I was going to pay for that. She barreled into me, and we both went sailing through the air, her fist clenching a wad of my hair.

I landed on my side with a whack.

So much for this being an uneventful party. The entertainment had just arrived. A small group had gathered around Amara and me, some watching with interest, others jeering on a chick fight. I'd hate to disappoint.

She grabbed hold of my arm, zapping me with a sharp bolt of electricity. The shock of it made my hair sizzle. I yelped. Of course Amara was the kind of girl who fought dirty, using not only a physical attack but also magic.

Two could play this game. I rolled, taking her with me, until I was on top.

"*Jesus Christ*," I heard Gavin swear. "Bri," he warned.

But in the haze of red cloudy my vision, I ignored

him. "My turn," I hissed between my teeth. With my free hand, I snatched her wrist and sent a stream of power right back. Except the moment I touched her, I could feel her magic, pulsating on the surface. My anger mixed with the tremor of her power—a volatile cocktail.

Gavin jumped up, throwing his arms around my waist, all amusement gone. "Calm down," he whispered softly in my ear, tearing me away from Amara. "Your eyes."

I pulled against his hold, but I didn't make it far. Lowering my hands, I balled them into fists at my side. People were staring at us, but I managed to keep myself from going all glow-eyes.

"You...you," Amara sputtered. She flipped the loose pieces of wet hair that had fallen in her face. "You're going to regret that," she seethed.

"Try me," I barked, seriously thinking about hitting someone for the first time in my life.

"I swear by the stars and the moons, I will destroy you."

Oh, goodie.

Chapter Four

That bitch.

I don't know who she thought she was messing with, but she had another thing coming if she thought she could intimidate me.

Gavin had his hand under my elbow, guiding me out into the street. Night reigned, the moon hemorrhaging overhead, dripping in crimson and gold. A blood moon was never a good omen.

As soon as we were outside, Austin threw his head back and laughed. "Holy shit, Bri, that was..."

"Reckless, stupid," Gavin interjected.

A frown pulled at my lips. He was right, but anger was still clouding my common sense.

"I was going to say really hot," Austin informed. He was more or less bouncing down the street alongside us. "I knew you were a tiger, but way to unleash your tigress."

My blood was still sizzling, but I let the evening breeze wash over my face and sucked in a breath of the crisp air. It helped. "I guess the party's over."

Gavin chuckled, weaving his fingers through mine. "Good grief, I can't leave you alone for five minutes. But at least we got what we wanted."

"And much more," Austin added, smirking. "A drink and a show. It's more than what I get on a first date."

I let a short laugh. "Sorry. I hope I didn't ruin your night."

"Are you kidding? That's the most fun I've had all week."

"Glad one of us enjoyed ourselves," I said, rubbing the side of my head, making sure I didn't have a bald spot. Amara had one hell of a grip.

Gavin's gaze snapped to mine, a slash of menace in the shadows. "I'm not even going to ask what happened back there, but stay clear of her, Bri. I know a witch with a vendetta, and that one has it out for you."

Unbidden, I took a step closer to him. There was something in the air, about this whole night that had me on edge. "What else is new?"

"Hold up. I know a shortcut." Austin forcible changed my direction.

Unease pricked down my spine. "A graveyard? Are you kidding me?"

"Wuss," Austin persisted, taking a step toward the cemetery. "Don't tell me you're superstitious?"

When Gavin didn't object, I wet my lips. "I'm a witch. Obviously, I'm superstitious, you idiot."

Austin grimaced.

A dark mist drifted over the uneven ground, blanketing the grass and marked graves. Austin filled the silence with nonsense chatter, reliving how I so expertly threw my drink in Amara's face. I just wanted to forget this night ever happened.

I was cursing Amara when something tight and inexorable tangled around my ankle and I stumbled. *Thump.* I went down with a scream, falling on my hands and knees. Clumps of dirt pitted under my fingernails. A few seconds went by before I got my bearings and realized the dark hole I was staring into was an open grave. The dirt was freshly turned over, as if someone had recently dug it.

A bone-chilling thought.

"What the heck," I mumbled.

Heart racing, I pushed the hair out of my face and lifted my head. Gavin helped me to my feet, and

I brushed the dirt and dust from my hands. At this rate, if I kept falling, I was going to be black and blue tomorrow.

Could this night get any worse?

Why yes, it could.

A moaning erupted a few feet from where I'd taken my less than graceful tumble. Gavin and I glanced at each other for a second, silently asking the other if they felt the sudden drop in temperature. If I thought I was cold before, now I could see the breath gather and freeze in front of my face.

His starlight eyes darkened. "Bri, we have a problem."

No shit, Sherlock. I was tired, achy, crabby, and so cold I thought my tits were going to freeze off. My teeth were starting to chatter as I looked up and saw a form emerging from the evening fog. The smell of rotting flesh wafted through the crisp air. I wrinkled my nose.

What the—

A twig snapped as a man trudged into a ray of moonlight. His clothes were dirty and ripped, eyes sunken and sagging, and his skin the color of toothpaste. Mud, leaves, and debris were scattered into his matted, stringy hair. I swear a chunk of his scalp was missing, but it could have been the light.

And then it hit me.

This dude was really, really dead.

I sucked in a breath, pushing to my feet. "Gavin?" My voice trembled slightly.

"Is this a joke?" Austin said backing up. "This better be a joke."

There was no time to process the surreal fact that this guy was a monster, and it wasn't a hallucination, because more bodies were climbing out of the ground.

Oh, God. This was a nightmare, right? Nope, this was the end of me, of us. There was no way we could fight so many. And my eyes were still having a hard time believing what I was seeing.

"Move!" Gavin railed.

The three of us spun around to go back the way we came, but ended up staring directly into the faces of four moaning monsters, their bones brittle and eroded.

"Shit," Gavin spat, eloquent as always.

Monsters. Monsters. And more monsters. They closed in around us, here, there, everywhere. A clammy sheen of fear slicked over my skin, mixed with the taste of acid in my mouth. Breathe in...breathe out...

"Bri, get behind me," Gavin ordered, always trying to be the hero. "And try not to get killed," he added.

Killed? I was just trying to avoid a panic attack. The thing was, there were too many for him to singlehandedly dispatch. He knew it. I knew it. Hell, even Austin knew it.

"Guys?" Austin said, quivering. His back touched mine.

Panting like I'd run a mile, I flipped out my hand, calling forth my power. "I guess running is off the table." I needed to be brave. It was easier to tell yourself to be something than actually *be* it.

When it came down to my friends, to those I cared about, I knew what had to be done. These things had to die. The wind picked up, howling like a pissed off banshee. Throwing my hand forward, I had a straight shot. A burst of bluish-white light exploded from my fingertips and body-slammed into one of the walking dead.

Black goo oozed from where I'd hit him, and the smell of burning corpse filled the air. Then to my great relief, the monster teetered on his rocky feet and fell to the ground. In what could only be magic, a black mist drifted over his body and it disintegrated into dirt. I didn't have time to appreciate how kickass that had felt.

"Bri!" Gavin roared.

"What?" I yelled, hardly believing he was going

to scold me at a time like this.

His blue eyes were shining with magic. "I told you to stay out of the way."

The putrid stench of death was everywhere, burning my nostrils. "We don't have time to argue. I'm doing this." I didn't claim to be an all-knowing witch, but with Gavin's help, I'd been able to learn a thing or two about using magic for other means. This was what I'd been trained for, to fight magic with magic. I could do this.

When he didn't argue, I let my power build inside me, holding nothing back. I arched, giving my arms more space. Gavin's green light streamed alongside mine as we sent blast after blast, sending the monsters back into the ground where they belonged. In dizzying intervals, the tiny light particles shimmered through the air, hitting the monsters, one after another. They weren't fast or smart, which helped.

Much to my shock, the three of us stood in the center of the graveyard, alone once again. Other than my scratched knees, no one got hurt. The dark mist faded, taking the quiver of magic with it. I rubbed my hands up and down my arms, attempting to chase the icy cold that had taken up residency. Strange.

I couldn't help thinking that the fight had been

too easy.

Something to contemplate later, I supposed. After we got out of here.

"What was in that drink?" Austin asked hoarsely.

My fingers were humming with the aftereffects of using so much magic. I couldn't seem to stop staring at the ground. Two fingers pressed under my chin, forcing my head up.

"You okay?" Gavin's voice softened, edged with concern.

I swallowed. "Yeah."

Dark hair toppled over his forehead. "Amara is a necromancer."

Chapter Five

"A necromancer?" I echoed, the second we were inside the dorms safe and sound, thanks to a protection spell. "You're shitting me!"

"I wish," Gavin said. Thick lashes shielded his eyes, but from the strain in his voice, it wasn't good.

"You mean like dark magic?"

He nodded. "She can raise the dead."

Crap on a graham cracker. "I didn't even know that was possible."

"There is a lot you still have to learn."

I moved my fingers, the tingles of magic finally ebbing off. "What makes you think it was her?" Don't get me wrong, I wasn't Amara's biggest fan, but it seemed biased to assume she was the witch responsible. Yes, she had a reason to get back at me, but she didn't strike me as someone smart enough to pull off the kind of spell required to raise the dead.

The dorm was quiet for a Friday night. Austin had gone up to his room. Too much excitement, he proclaimed. Gavin raked a hand through his hair. "Remember how I've said that magic has a distant signature? It's kind of like a scent or a stamp. Like Sophie can see auras, I can see Amara's autograph all over those guys. It was her. I got a quick glimpse of her magic when she zapped you earlier."

"Ugh, don't remind me," I said, sinking down onto my bed and kicking off my flip-flops. College no longer seemed like the safest place. If she could raise the dead, what else could this witch do?

Nothing good came to mind.

"Geez, all I did was throw my drink on her." I couldn't imagine what the repercussions would have been if I'd done something truly wicked. She clearly hadn't been joking about destroying me.

Gavin jammed his hands into his pockets. "It's the darkness. It feeds into a witch's emotions, twisting the mind. She's more dangerous than she appears. Don't let her fool you. And keep your guard up around that one. I have a feeling tonight was only a warning. She's showing us what she can do."

"I get it. She's the big witch on campus. I'm not looking to get her way or be part of her little coven. I've never been a groupie." The frustration was evident in my tone.

Gavin stared at me, his jaw curving. "You know, Austin was right."

Tiling my head back and forth, I worked out the stress kinks in my neck. My brow crinkled. "About what?" I asked.

A glimmer of mischief crossed his expression. "It was hot."

I rolled my eyes. "You're warped."

"And you're cute when you're all worked up."

"If you think that was cute, just wait until you see what I have planned next."

He tugged on the ends of my hair, rocking back on his heels. "Honestly, I don't know if I should be intrigued or scared shitless."

"Probably a little of both." I noticed the empty bed on the other side of the room. My roommate, Kylie, was out for the night. She had a boyfriend a few floors above. The chances of her coming home tonight were slim. "Did you put that protection spell on your room?" I asked.

Gavin cast a sideway glance. "Um, of course."

"Good. I don't want to have to worry about Austin." Something came over me. Maybe it was the near death experience. I more or less tackled Gavin, throwing myself at him. "Stay," I whispered, raining kisses over his cheeks and chin.

His eyes roamed over my face in a slow perusal. "What took you so long?" he whispered, backing me into a wall and making me gasp. His gaze centered on my lips, before he closed the little distance between us.

My pulse exploded. So hot, his kiss short-circuited my brain. I wasn't thinking of anything but him in that moment. Amara and her monsters was the furthest thing from my mind.

Wonderfully dazed, I couldn't get close enough. His lips meshed against mine, his tongue sliding into my mouth. Sweeping his arms around my waist, we landed on my bed. Our legs tangled as his body pressed into me, and somehow my hands ended up under his shirt, my nails marking his skin. Shivers raced up and down my spine, and I clung to him like ivy.

He pushed the sleeve down my collarbone, exposing my skin and pressed his lips to my shoulder. "Promise me you'll be careful," he murmured.

"I can take care of myself," I assured. There was

no need for him to worry. He taught me to be cautious, and how to use magic to defend myself.

"I know you can, but it only takes one careless mistake. Don't make a mistake."

My fingers dug into his shirt. "I don't want to talk about her. Actually, I don't want to talk at all."

Gavin brushed my hair back, his fingers lingering over my cheeks. "What did she say to piss you off?"

"It was stupid," I said, lowering my lashes.

"That wasn't an answer," he insisted.

"I saw her hitting on you and...I lost it."

He leaned forward, sweeping his lips over mine. "You're amazing."

My mouth tingled from his kisses, making my belly flipped. "That's what I've been telling you."

He chuckled against my mouth. "What am I going to do with you?"

"I can think of a few things," I replied, twisting in his embrace and placing a soft kiss on his lips. He ran his fingers lightly over my hip, returning the kiss. There was a tenderness that made me ache.

But the thing with Gavin, he always left me breathless. One minute he was sweet and gentle and the next, my hands were captive over my head as he changed angles, deepening the kiss. He left me no choice but to meet him heat for heat. The weight of him was delicious.

Growing impatient, I wanted the feel of him against me, skin to skin, no barriers, nothing getting in the way. I sat up and raised my arms. Gavin didn't hesitate. Bunching his fingers at the hem of my shirt, he lifted it over my head. His was next, joining mine on the floor.

With nothing standing in our way, his hands roamed everywhere, along my slender neck, down the curve of my shoulder, over the dip of my stomach. I sucked in a sharp breath and bit my lip as he followed each touch with a whisper of a kiss. The metal of his lip ring cooled my scorched flesh.

I was positive that at this point in my life, there was no other moment as perfect as this. Maybe it was the walking corpses. Maybe it was Amara. Maybe it was the thought of losing him.

Regardless of the reasons that propelled me, all that mattered was that he was here, with *me*. "I love you," I whispered.

His eyes were radiating, casting a starry light into the darkness. "Not as much as I love you."

I wound my arms around his neck, reaching for him. "Don't think about stopping," I said in case he had any ideas.

He flashed me a grin, his head dipping. "I wouldn't dream of it." Then he was kissing me again.

My body flushed, and my heart was pounding too fast. I could feel his beating with mine.

This was true love.

This was magic.

Chapter Six

I was in line at the small coffee shop on campus, rocking a pair of dark shades to cover the circles under my eyes. The last few nights had been restless. Even with Gavin lying beside me, I hadn't gotten much sleep—if any.

I spent the weekend holed up in the dorm, catching up on homework and binge watching Netflix with Austin and Gavin. But no matter how much drama there was on TV, it paled in comparison to my real life. I was hiding out, not only because I didn't want to have a run-in with Amara, but also because I was embarrassed by my behavior.

What had come over me?

Jealousy was an exhausting emotion, and one I wasn't proud of acting out on. My anger had always been a trigger for me, evoking my powers before I even knew I had them. It had made for a very interesting childhood.

Sometimes it was hard to ignore how effortless it would be to simply extract Amara's magic. Why did it always require more effort to be good than to be bad? Knowing Amara used black magic made me want to stop her. That kind of power was no joke. I knew firsthand the consequences and allure dark magic had. Like a drug, it was addictive to the point of self-destruction.

Or in my case, soul destruction.

As I waited for my caramel macchiato, I thought about skipping astronomy. The prospect of seeing Amara's face gave me hives, in no small part because I was afraid of what I might do. As much as I practiced control, I wasn't feeling extremely confident today in my ability to resist the urge. If she provoked me, I was afraid I would strike back in the one way I knew would truly stop her.

"Brianna," the barista called my name.

I grabbed my cup of joe and glanced at the clock. There was still twenty minutes before class started, so I found an empty seat in the corner. Digging out my phone, I passed the time scrolling through my Facebook feed. Sophie had posted a silly picture from Homecoming.

I sipped my drink, feeling a bit nostalgic. Seeing her face made me think of home and Aunt Clara. I made a mental note to call her tonight, to check in and make sure she was remembering to eat.

"Bippity-boppity-boo," a voice sang behind me.

My fingers tightened around the warm paper cup and I closed my eyes. *For the love of God.* I lifted my head, meeting Amara's cool light green eyes. "Are you stalking me?" I accused. Probably not the best way to start a conversation, but this chick was trying my patience.

Her dark denim jeans were painted on as she slid into the empty seat across from me. "You wish."

My hands flattened on the table. "Since you're not drinking coffee, what is it you want, Amara?"

She giggled, clearly taking sick pleasure in tormenting me. "Did you enjoy the party?"

Yep. She got her rocks off screwing with me. What a witch. And that wasn't a compliment. "Honestly, it was kind of *stiff*." Like those walking dead bodies, I added silently.

The fake-ass smile on her lips flinched ever so slightly. "I'm a little surprised. I sort of thought you'd be the kind of witch who would dabble on the other side. You're not exactly Glenda the Good Witch, are you?"

Unease rose swiftly, snaking its way inside me. "What are you talking about? Why would you think that?"

"Call it a talent. You might look like peaches and cream on the outside, but inside, you're not as innocent as you portray."

I pressed my knees together under the table. My palms were beginning to sweat. "I don't screw with the dark arts," I said, keeping my voice low. "And if you knew what's good for you, you wouldn't either. But then again, you don't strike me as the wisest wand in the shop."

She crossed her legs and leaned back in the chair. The soft pendant light from the coffee shop picked up the sheen from her satin shirt. "If you say so, but the craft doesn't lie, Brianna. Humans do, but magic, it doesn't discriminate."

Amara was more perceptive than I'd given her credit for. Gavin was right. I needed to be very, very cautious around her. Already, I got the impression she knew more than I was comfortable with. And don't even get me started about the way the girl dressed. Who the hell wore spiked heels and tight jeans to an 8:00 a.m. class? She looked insanely hot, which burned my butt. I was lucky if I swept a coat of mascara over my eyes. Forget about doing my hair. I was rocking a fashion-forward messy bun. "What's your deal? I thought you wanted to destroy me."

Her lips thinned. "Oh, I still do. But...I also admire a girl who doesn't take shit."

"Look, I don't want to upset your throne. I get it. You're some big shot on campus. Just so we're straight, I don't use my gifts to manipulate people."

A flash of silver popped in her eyes. I was getting to her, not necessarily a good thing. "You don't know the first thing about me."

"I know enough to not want to join your sorority." Glancing at the clock, I had less than five minutes to get to class. Time to wrap this riveting conversation up. "Is there a point to this visit, or are you here to annoy me?"

Her long nails rapped over the tabletop. "Both. Annoying you is just a bonus, an entertaining one. But there is something I want."

My mouth dried. "Oh, and what might that be?" I asked, but was afraid I already knew.

"As cute as your boyfriend is, I'm more interested in you."

My mouth nearly hit the table. "You want me?" I squeaked. I didn't know whether I should be flattered or completely freaked out. "I think it's pretty clear I don't play for the other side. I have a boyfriend."

She laughed, sexy and husky. I could never pull off a laugh like that. "You're not my type either, doll."

All I could do was lift my brows. I was at a loss for words.

"I want you in my sorority," she replied.

I choked. "In your coven," I corrected. "One minute you're trying to kill me, and the next you're trying to recruit me. I think you need to get your head examined."

A bitter laugh snuck out. "Sarcastic and funny. You're like a triple threat."

"Except, I'm not a threat." *Yet...*I added to myself.

"Listen, Brianna, I got a taste of the amount of power you keep in check. I can help, you know, tap into all that power. There is more to magic than gimmicks and hexes. I can show you." There was an undeniable eagerness in her voice.

"I already have a mentor," I said dryly.

She tipped her head, copper curls falling to one side. "Your boyfriend, as hot as he is, doesn't have the amount of juice you do. His abilities are limited. I, on the other hand, can show you magic you've never imagined."

"Thanks, but I'll take my chances with Gavin." I trusted him. We'd been through some serious crap together. Amara, I barely knew, and not to mention, she had unleashed a group of walking corpses on me. I wouldn't call that exactly trustworthy.

"You're making a huge mistake," she insisted.

Man, I was starting to think this witch didn't understand the word no. "It's mine to make. Why would you want to help me? What's in it for you?" I shot back.

"As sisters, we support each other. Our circle makes us stronger. Haven't you ever heard of camaraderie?"

My stomach tumbled over. I tried to swallow, but a god-awful lump formed in the back of my throat. "I don't get along well with others."

Fire crackled in her eyes. "I've heard some pretty lame excuses, but yours take the cake."

"Okay, how about this. No. Is that plain enough for you?" I gathered my books and drink. Amara and I were done here. I had nothing else to say to her.

"I don't take no. Eventually, I'll wear you down."

I jerked my head up. "How? By threatening me?"

She shrugged. "I'm used to getting what I want."

"I don't know what you think you'll gain from having me in your coven, but I promise you, there is nothing you can do or say that will change my mind. I'm not here to gain power or join a coven. I just want a degree." I stood and started for the door.

"We'll see about that. I can be very persuasive," she said, following me out the door and across the yard to the science building.

I said nothing as I power-walked. She was hot on my heels. Throwing open the door, I briefly contemplated casting a quick spell to lock the double doors, but she'd probably undo it faster than I could conjure.

Her bombshell-red lips curled. "You can run, Brianna, but you can't escape your destiny."

"I've already meet my destiny," I replied coldly, turning the handle to room 103.

Everyone turned to look as Amara and I burst into the classroom, making enough noise to start a stampede. I wanted to duck under a table. I could feel my cheeks starting to burn. Being the center of attention sucked. Amara however, seemed to thrive on disruptive nature.

"Ladies, is there a problem?" Professor Burns asked, as we had walked in on his lecture. Class had started.

All I could think as I slinked to my seat was, *only one. Amara.*

Chapter Seven

A dark cluster of clouds moved in front of the moon, mirroring my current mood: glum and despondent. North Carolina was having unseasonably cold weather for this time of year. I hunkered down in my UNCW hoodie as the wind whipped around me. Gold and rust colored leaves fell from the trees, spiraling to the ground.

Austin let out a stream of hot air. "Christ, it's colder than an Eskimo pie."

I shivered. "Don't even think about suggesting another shortcut," I warned him.

"I can't believe I let you talk me into going to the library."

I matched our footsteps, keeping my arms wrapped around me. "Do you want to actually pass a class?"

"Why do think I am trudging it across campus in this kind of weather? If I don't pass *all* my classes, you can kiss my sorry ass goodbye."

His parents were stickler about grades. If he didn't hold at least a 3.0 GPA, he would be paying for college out of his own pocket.

Austin pulled his Neff beanie down over his ears. "Can't you do something about the weather? I mean, this is ridiculous."

I frowned. "I am doing something."

Tipping his head back, he glanced up at the sky. "Wow, Bri, what the heck is up your butt?"

"You know I can't always control it."

"Well, whatever it is, can you hurry up and get happy? I want to see the sun. And I really hate knowing you're in a rut. Do you want a hug?" Whether I did or not, Austin didn't give me a choice. His arms wiggled through mine. "Or maybe a big, fat slice of warm apple pie with a scoop of vanilla ice cream? It works for me."

I leaned my head on his shoulder. His body heat chased the chill. "I wish it were that simple. I miss Aunt Clara and Tori. I know it's only an hour away, but lately it feels like I'm living on the other side of the universe."

"I know what you mean. We should take ourselves on a little road trip this weekend," he suggested.

I nodded. He was right. I really needed a weekend at home, in my own bed.

"Maybe we can even get that slice of pie."

I laughed.

In spite of the weirdness that was my life, I felt at peace the moment I stepped into the library. Books of every shape, size, and color lined the walls. Dusty ones or new books with their seams still intact, it didn't matter, I loved them all. There was this little breath of happiness that filled me, taking a way a sliver of the homesickness.

The library was deader than Amara's corpses, just the way I liked it. Despite Austin's procrastination and grumbling, we got to work. His study ethics were very different than mine. Earbuds in, he repeatedly tapped the end of his pencil with the beat of his playlist.

"How do you retain any information like that?" I whispered.

"Huh?" he answered in a volume louder than his inside voice.

"Sshh," I scolded, putting my finger to my lips.

His eyes widened in understanding, and he

pulled out the cord from his ears. "Oh yeah, like there is anyone to disturb."

"There's me," I said drily.

"That's because you're the only idiot dumb enough to traipse around in this kind of weather, and I'm the moron who agreed to go with you."

I rolled my eyes.

"So, where's hotpants at?" Austin asked, referring to Gavin.

My lips twitched at the corners. "I would pay to see you call him that to his face."

He drummed his pencil against his lips, contemplating. "It might be worth the risk of being zapped by magic."

I grinned. "He's meeting Jared to see if they can dig up any info on necromancers and Amara's sorority."

"Boy is paranoid, but again, he has a right to be. Seen any corpses wandering around campus lately?"

I exhaled. "No, thank God." "The one time was enough for me."

"Does hotpants still think it was she-who-may-not-be-named?"

"For sure. I just can't figure what her angle is. She's wants my power, but for what? That's what has got Gavin on edge."

"Which is precisely why I'm sticking to you like

white on rice, girlfriend."

My gaze tapered. "Did Gavin ask you to come with me today?" I inquired, suspecting that my overprotective boyfriend didn't want me to be left alone. This had his signature all over it.

Austin turned his head to the side, running his hand along the back of his neck. "I know nothing about that."

I pursed my lips. "Uh-huh."

The two seats across the table were suddenly no longer empty. Willow and Ophelia occupied the seats, making themselves comfortable in their matching KZG hoodies. Austin and I looked at each other with the same WTH glances.

I cleared my throat.

Smiling slightly, Ophelia dropped her backpack on the floor. "Hey."

"Hey," I replied. "Ophelia, right? We meet at the party the other night."

She nodded. "Yeah, when you dumped your drink over Amara."

I had a feeling, that one incident was going to follow me through all four years of college. "Um, that was sort of a misunderstanding."

Her shoulders gave a shrug. "We get it. Amara can be a bitch sometimes."

"Sometimes?" I repeated, unable to keep the

disbelief from my voice.

"Okay, maybe once or twice a day," Willow amended.

"Or more like every hour," Austin mumbled, eyes staring down at his open textbook.

"True, she isn't the easiest person to get along with, but she'll be the first one to stick up for you."

Austin nudged me with his elbow. "Sounds like someone else I know."

I scowled, more or less ignoring him. "Let me guess. She sent you guys here to convince me to join your sorority?"

Willow winked. "That obvious, huh?"

Amara had warned me she was relentless. "I'm pretty sure nothing Amara does is subtle."

Willow put up a hand. "Before you say no, all we ask is that you come by and check out the house, meet some of the girls, see what we're all about before you make up your mind about KZG. I'm sure you have this preconceived notion of what you think our sorority is like. We'd like you to give us the chance to show you we're not a cult. We're sisters. A family. We help each other. We support one another."

I believed Willow and Ophelia truly believed that, and maybe it was true, but I'd gotten a glimpse of the darker side of Amara. She had a game plan. I wouldn't be surprised if the whole sorority was part of a larger scheme. My gut was telling me not to trust Amara.

They read the doubt on my face. "No parties. Just the sorority sisters," Ophelia added.

"You guys have a really strange way of recruiting members," Austin rebutted. "Unleashing an army of—"

I kicked him under the table. Austin, Gavin, and I knew what Amara had done in the graveyard, but I wasn't sure if her sorority sisters knew the kind of magic she conjured. "What Austin is trying to say is that Amara and I haven't exactly gotten off on the right foot."

"Well, you must have done something to impress her. She's never works this hard to get someone into the cov...sorority," Willow corrected.

Clearly, they weren't sure how much Austin knew of my world. "I hope Amara appreciates the friends she has, and I'm sorry you wasted your Saturday."

"There's nothing we can do to change your mind?" Ophelia asked, one last attempt to get me to change my mind.

I gritted my teeth and shoved my books into my bag. "Austin, let's go."

Chapter Eight

Rush week.

Someone shoot me now.

It was hard to ignore all the house colors every other student wore, and the clutter of streamers and flyers being handed out at the dorms.

But I was doing my damnedest.

The only way Amara was going to get me into house KZG was kicking and screaming. Now that the thought crossed my mind, I wouldn't put it past her. I glanced over my shoulder to make sure no one was following me as I exited the math building.

Paranoid much?

Any anxiety I was feeling dissipated the moment

I set eyes on Gavin. He was lazily leaning against the brick building, looking so content. Faint traces of stubble shadowed his jaw as he lifted his head up, and when he looked at me like that, his eyes most definitely twinkled. He had a disheveled-from-sleep sexiness I couldn't resist. You would think that after a year, I wouldn't get giddy and excited every time he looked at me. I did. Fireflies zoomed in my belly, warm and charged.

My lips curved. I stood on my toes and pressed my lips to his. "Is it your turn to babysit me?"

Gavin tipped his head down, smirking. "First off, wanting to spend time with my girlfriend is not babysitting."

My arms went around his neck. "You know, nothing has happened since the night of the party. Maybe she isn't up to anything. Maybe she was just feeling slighted and vindictive that night."

He kissed the tip of my nose. "Maybe hell has frozen over."

I looped my arm through his, doing a mental eye roll. "Fine. I get it. You're still skeptical."

Putting an around my shoulder, he tucked me into his side as we started walking to the dorm. "Give her time. She'll dig her own grave."

The warmth of him quickly seeped into my bones. I smacked him on the chest. "Funny. Maybe you should quit school and become a comedian."

His sapphire eyes sparkled under the waning light. "Who would keep you out of trouble?"

He had a point. It felt good to be nestled up against him, safe, after I'd slogged through two classes today. "Trouble does seem to find me no matter where I hide. Have you figured what she's up to?" Like many of our conversations, we someone how circled back to Amara.

He shook his head. "Not yet."

I made my steps match his long strides as he ate up the ground. "That's a good thing, right?"

Brows knitting, a bothered expression settled on his face. "Not necessarily."

The wind whined and groaned in the distance. *Wait, what?* It wasn't even windy. If the wind wasn't making those noises, then...

I stiffened, jerking to a halt. "Did you hear that?"

The muscle at his jaw ticked. "Yeah, but I'm really hoping it was some drunk frat douche."

I snuggled closer to him. "Me, too."

The moan sounded again, but this time was followed by a high-pitch scream.

Shit.

Every inch of Gavin's body went on high alert. I placed a hand on his arm, needing to touch him. "Drunk or not, someone is screaming in fear," I said, knowing I couldn't stand here and pretend I didn't hear them. I spun around. The air was stale in my lungs as I listened to pinpoint which direction it was coming from.

My eyes brightened, narrowing in the direction of the grassy section behind the library, toward the...

You've got to be kidding me. The cemetery! Again!

Now I positively knew what those groans were— the dead being raised.

My eyes were large as saucers when I turned back to Gavin, peering at him. "We need to do something."

His gaze was steely. "Yeah, we do. I need to get you out of here."

"Gavin!" I protested when his fingers wrapped around mine, tugging me down the path away from the screams.

"Hell, no. You're not running straight into a graveyard filled with zombies."

I dug my heels in and planted my weight, refusing to take another step in the wrong direction. "You're going to have to drag me, then."

"That can be arranged." Stealth-mode Gavin appeared. "You're going to the dorm."

"I'm not leaving," I shouted. Little good it did.

He moved. His shoulder dipped as he placed his hands on my hips to hoist me over his shoulder. "Why do you always insist on arguing with me? Just once, will you do as I ask?"

Not today. "I'm not leaving you alone. We both know you can't walk away," I said, dangling in the air. I grabbed onto his shirt, my hair flying in my face.

"I didn't think so," he answered himself, and took a step or two away from the cries.

"It could be someone we know. It could be Austin."

He paused, and I knew I'd won. Then he huffed, his chest rising and falling heavily underneath me. "What are we waiting for?" he grumbled, sounding resigned. His fingers ran up to my hips.

"Thank you," I said a soon as my feet touched the ground. If there had been time, I would have kissed him.

He angled his head at me, eyeing me with disbelief. "You know, you won't always get your way."

My lips twitched. That was debatable. My amusement was short-lived. Another long and tortured scream rang, louder and more frantic. "Hurry. We've got to stop them before they hurt someone!"

"If they haven't already," he said grimly.

And that was probably what Amara wanted. I had a bad, bad feeling about this. We were walking into a trap, but what else could we do? We couldn't let those things run around. If we didn't stop them, there was no telling how many people might get hurt...or worse.

It was always the *or worse* that made me prickly.

Chapter Nine

I wasn't fond of the dead....or the cemetery, for that matter.

Together we raced toward the cries. As I ran, I conjured my magic, preparing for the worse. When I reached the edge of the hill, I stumbled and came to a dead stop, Gavin skidding beside me.

It was almost too much to take in. The entire lot not far from the school campus was covered with about a dozen monsters, with more scratching and clawing out of the ground. And in the middle of monster mash pit was... I craned my neck, trying to get a better look without drawing attention our way. The dead hadn't noticed the arrival of two witches, and it would be in our best interest to keep it that way, get the jump on them.

To my utter relief, it wasn't Austin being cornered by the dead. It was Willow. *Seriously.*

There was no time to process the surreal fact that Amara put one of her own sorority sisters in danger. Then again, it shouldn't have surprised me.

Right now, I had to fight, to put the skills Gavin had taught me to good use. I couldn't allow Gavin to deal with the monsters himself. For a panicked moment, I realized I didn't have a weapon, and then I remembered: I was a witch; magic was my sword.

Breathe...in...breathe...out.

The therapeutic exercise didn't really help.

While I was having a semi-breakdown, Gavin jumped right in. When he fought using magic, it was as if he became a different person—a different version of himself. The one standing in front of me now was fierce and cold, a warrior. It was a calculated move, putting himself in the line of fire and giving me time to collect myself.

He conjured a bow, equipped with glowing green arrows. He extended the bow and launched an arrow straight for Willow. At the last second, the monster surged ahead in the direct path of the arrow. It sliced across its throat, spraying bits of flesh. The entire creature's body shuddered, and then he just sort of stopped, his body exploding in darkmist that spread over the ground. The dust hadn't even settled, and Gavin was locking and loading for round two.

A moan sounded from behind me. It was my time to shine. I whirled. Two monsters decided to join the massacre bash and another one was digging himself out of his grave. Lighting up my hands, I tossed an electric ball of power at the closest one. His black orbs glazed before he gave a feral howl and burst into mist. One down, and more than we could handle left.

These things had to die.

I took a deep breath, steadying myself and launched forward. My fist went through the air, packed with magic as the next one reached me. On contact, a wave of energy fizzled through my veins and the monster went kaboom.

It felt good.

Apparently, I could do this.

I arched back, giving my power time to rejuvenate before slamming my palm into the next creature's nose. This was a female, except the bitch didn't disintegrate. *What the hell.* The creature grabbed me, latching onto my arms, scratching me with its jagged, dirty claws. Panic set in.

I twisted, kicked, and bucked, basically anything I could think of to loosen this thing's grasp. One of my blows landed in the creature's stomach, propelling her backward. She went to the ground, but another one took her place. It would only be a minute before she was back on her feet and going for my throat.

Hands extended, the walking dead snarled and hissed inaudible noises that reminded me of tortured animals.

Like a puff of hot air, I blasted a sphere of magic, not wanting another up close and personal encounter. Not only did these things smell to high heaven, they were faster than they were previously. Then again, it was magic giving them life.

Taking a second to find Gavin, I was relieved to see he was up and fighting. He moved with fluid grace, bending out of the way when a creature lunged, only to circle around and blast them from behind.

He had made his way to Willow, and was trying to keep the monsters off of them both. But the moment they had a clear path, Willow took off, darting into the woods. And that left Gavin and I in the thick of it.

Typical. That's the thanks we get for saving her life.

As soon as I made it out of here alive, I was going to march down to that stupid witchcraft sorority house and give Willow the tongue lashing of a lifetime. What a dick move, leaving us there.

But the battle raged on. The more we fought, the more excited they seemed to become. The faster my heart pounded, the faster they moved. It was an endless cycle.

But I had to survive.

I had to stop Amara, and there was only one way I knew how. All I had to do was make my way to her, and to do that, I needed to battle my way through the army of monsters she called upon.

"Why don't you fight me yourself?" I yelled into the air. Instead she sent her bony and decayed goons.

Her response was the converging of four monsters.

I backed up, shooting a series of blasts—a glow here, a glow there. Grunts and moans came from all around me.

One of the monsters snuck up behind me and managed to shackle my ankle with his skeletal fingers. Unbelievable. His grip was so strong, I couldn't break free, and he tugged me to the ground, but not before I blasted the last of the group with a beam of magic.

As soon as I hit the ground, I was kicking and twisting, doing whatever I could to free myself. But no matter how hard I struggled, I couldn't break away. It was just one monster, but it was as though he had the strength and weight of a thousand. I fought and fought and fought as the thing clawed at my face and ripped at my clothes. He barred his teeth, trying to take a chunk out of my neck.

I screamed.

An instant later, Gavin was behind the bastard. He reached around, flattening his palm over the monster's heart. A green light erupted between them, so it intense it was blinding.

I blinked. Gavin was hovering over me, and we were both panting and sweating. "Stay quiet," he whispered, carefully securing his hands under my upper arms and hauling me to my feet.

I glanced at him. It was not surprising that he fared far better than I had, with only a nick on his cheek and a bruise.

"Are you okay?" he asked. He was still holding me, making sure I wasn't going to crumble back to the ground.

I nodded. "I'm fine." A tremor moved down my spine. But I couldn't say the same about Amara, when I got my paws on her. The longer I stood there leaning on Gavin, seeing the pain and destruction she caused, for no good reason, the more my blood boiled. "I'm going to kill her," I rasped, eyes burning violet.

Gavin's gaze narrowed. "I agree she needs to be stopped, but I don't think we have to resort to murder."

"You know what I mean. I'm not going to literally kill her." It was a proclamation I meant to keep.

"Oh, good. Just so were clear." Concern rightfully clouded his eyes. "Are you sure you want to do that?"

We started at each other, the ground littered with the darkmist of the dead. What I was proposing wasn't to be taken lightly. There would be consequences if I took Amara's power—serious-no-take-back repercussions, but she had to be stopped. It became clear raising the dead wasn't a one-time thing for Amara. I needed to make sure tonight was the last time, and I would deal with the fallout once I knew she was no longer a threat.

I looked him in the eyes. "Yeah. I have to."

He might not like my choice, but he would support me. Always. "Well, let's go get us a witch."

I stepped back, more than ready to blow this dead zone. My fingers were intertwined with Gavin's as I swung around, giving him a tug, but something stopped him, his body firm.

Bri!" Gavin screamed.

My head whipped around at the sound of the sheer panic in his voice. There was a flare of fireworks sparking in front of my eyes. Beautiful. Mesmerizing. Bright.

I blinked.

And before my brain could compute what was happening, blackness descended.

Chapter Ten

I woke up tied to a chair, with music blaring in the background, no doubt to mask my screams. The bindings that held me weren't chains or loops of rope, but the magical kind, paralyzing my hands behind the chair and bolting my feet to the floor. Icy fear trickled down my spine.

Is that Madonna?

The pop acoustics of Material Girl pumped through the room at volumes that I hadn't attempted since I was thirteen.

Wow. Someone had a weird complex for Eighties music.

As my eyes adjusted to the candlelit room, I

took stock of my surroundings, anything to keep my mind from panicking over the fact I was restrained. The first thing I noticed was that the room was windowless, with no natural light to tell me how long I'd been unconscious. There was a damp coolness to the air, like the room was a basement or partially underground.

I looked down at my feet, willing them to move. Nothing happened. Fear and frustration tore through me, and I shuddered. I looked for something I could use, anything to aid my escape, when I noticed something unusual.

Runes.

They were charred into the hardwood floors, symbols I didn't recognize. I knew they were runes, but what kind. Protection? Traps? Summoning? My knowledge of runes and the ability of them were extremely lacking. I'd only just recently learned of the magical symbols—tools of the craft. There was so much to learn. Just when I thought I was wrapping my head around this witch stuff, I discovered I had barely broken the surface.

Red pillar candles flickered around the circle, with me tied in the center. At least I knew the properties of burning red candles. Danger. Channeling. Strength.

And then I saw it. Or him. A body lay just to

the right of my eyesight within the circle from me, unmoving and pale as a ghost. I wasn't all that shocked Amara had a dead dude in her house; it was the green misty glow surrounding his body from head to toe that gave me pause for concern. A spell. But what kind of spell?

If I had to guess...a preservation charm. A spell that preserved the body after someone had died and their soul had moved on.

My throat felt as if it was going to close up. The picture was suddenly becoming crystal clear in my head. Amara was channeling the power of her sorority sisters to try to bring someone back from the dead. All those zombies had been practice, but to restore more than a body, she would need an exuberant amount of power.

Oh God, please let me be wrong. If that was Amara's end game, then I understood what she needed me for. She needed more power. And I had enough to blow the roof off this place.

Forget regulating my breathing. It was coming out in short, hard pants that I couldn't seem to control. The scent of melting wax and expensive perfume filtered through the room, burning my nose.

"Good. You're awake."

My body locked up at the sound of the familiar

voice. I tried to twist in the chair so I could see her with my own eyes, but the invisible knots on my hands and feet prevented it.

"How are you feeling?" Amara asked. She came into my eyesight, candlelight flickering shadows on the side of her face.

I blinked, focusing on the belittling curve on her lips. "I'd feel a whole lot better if I wasn't tied to a seat."

She crossed her arms and put a single finger to her lips. "It does seem a bit extreme, but in my defense, I did try to get you here without the theatrics. You didn't make it easy."

"Relentless," I laughed, the freaked-out-scared-shitless-shrilly kind of laugh. "I guess you weren't kidding."

She blinked, and the look she gave me sent chills up my back. "I have plans for you, little witch. Big plans. You're the last piece I need...what I've been waiting for. And to think when I'd lost all hope, you practically fell at my feet."

"Plans? What plans?" My voiced was pitched high with fear.

"You'll see," she announced, a demented excitement in her voice. "Don't worry. You'll be fine. I'm not a serial killer or anything."

Her words did nothing to ease the terror

seizing me. "Good to know."

She walked the rim of the circle. "The other girls will be here soon, and then before you know it, this will all be over. Nothing but a memory, and you can trot back home to your boyfriend."

Gavin? Oh, my God. He'd been with me when I'd lost consciousness. "Where is he? What did you do with him?" I demanded, the fear I was feeling turned to anger, making my tone gravelly. If she'd hurt him...

Well, she didn't want to find out what I would do to her if one hair were harmed on his body.

"Your boy toy is fine, at least he was when we left him comatose in the cemetery," her green eyes focused on mine. "I'm sure my loyal minions are taking good care of him. His head might be throbbing, and he could be a little disoriented when he wakes up, but other than that, he'll live."

I fought against the bands of magic, but it was pointless. They didn't give, and I hadn't expected them too. "If you're lying," I seethed, nearly foaming at the mouth.

She lifted her chin. "Everything I've told you has been the truth."

"But not the whole truth," I interjected. "Whatever you're planning to do, Amara, I won't let you."

She smiled in a not so friendly way. "You don't have a choice."

The hell I didn't. There was always a choice. Amara had no idea who she was dealing with, or the kind of witch I was. These binds might physically hold me, but it wouldn't contain my magic. She had another think coming if she thought I was going to stand by and be a puppet in her spell.

I let out a shaky breath. "I have more power than you know."

She made a dismissive gesture, like I was nothing but an annoying fly buzzing in her ear. "That's what I'm counting on. You're not the only one who would do anything for someone you love. I understand the lengths you're willing to go, to protect Gavin. More than you know."

"I understand love, and how hard it must be losing someone you love. Who was it you lost?" I asked.

"No one that concerns you," she barked. "That's all you need to know."

Holy crap. I knew in my gut, I was right. The pieces fell into place. She was going to try and bring someone back from the dead. One thing I learned was, just because magic could do all sorts of phenomenal things, doesn't mean it was right. "I see a guy in my crystal ball," I replied, part smartass, part investigator.

"Enough!" she snapped, clenching her fists. The candles in the room flickered before the flame shot up, quadrupling in size and washing the room in burning glow. Someone had an anger management problem. That I understood.

I flinched before the candles returned to normal soft light, darkening the room.

After a calming breath, her gaze jerked to the corner of the room. As far as I could tell, nothing was there, but when her eyes began to glimmer in the dark, I things were about to get real. "The moon is high and full. It's time," she said, more to herself than me.

Time for what? It looked like I was about to find out.

She spun around, and footsteps sounded behind me. One by one, her fellow sorority sisters and witches came into the room, include Ophelia and Willow. If I wasn't tied to this chair, I would have flown out of the seat, straight at Willow, for her part in this shenanigan. Sitting around the drawn circle, they joined hands, beginning and ending with Amara.

An electric shock trembled in the air as soon as the circle was complete. The room was swathed in a reddish light, and within seconds, the temperature in the room went to subzero. A chill radiated over my body. My blood pressure accelerated, and the tightening in my chest couldn't be a good sign.

Power gripped me, and my head tipped back. Frustration bounced around inside my already tightened gut. I was unable to stop it. I pulled against my binds, to no avail. *What a bunch of cuckoo witches*, I added silently to myself.

Amara and her followers began the chant to what I recognized as a channeling spell. They were allowing Amara to borrow their gifts. Tonight was one of those times it sucked to be right. The other girls had power, but it was mediocre. Amara herself had more than the lot of them put together, but not as much as I had. I had given her a chance to be reasonable, and she was a fool if she thought her magic would hold me.

Forcing my body to relax, I took control of my gift, trying to calm the spark that begged to be unleashed. A boom of thunder crackled outside. "If you think using magic is the answer, than you're a bigger fool than I took you for. All of you," I ranted in a last desperate attempt make them see the mistake they were about to embark. "Dark magic comes with a price. It's dangerous and destructive. Whoever you're trying to bring back, this isn't the way. It's not natural. Not even magic can reverse death."

"Thanks for the buzzkill," Amara snarled. "Now keep quiet so I can concentrate. I wouldn't want to screw up the spell and hurt someone." Her insinuation was clear. If I didn't cooperate, Gavin would pay the price. "I'm only going to borrow a bit of magic. No harm done. You'll only be a bit tired. I'd prescribe lots of rest for the next few days."

Her sarcasm was stale. "You can breathe life into a dead body, Amara, but you can't give him his soul back."

She closed her eyes, ignoring me, as she channeled power from her circle. The other girls were as still as statues. Again, I felt her magic weave its way into me. This was it. I had to do something. Now. Before it was too late and I lost myself to the dark pull. "Listen to me closely, Amara. Stop this spell and close the circle."

Her voice only grew louder and stronger as she pushed the spell forward.

I'd given her a shot. One was all she got, and it was evident, she wanted to do this the hard way. I was going to siphon her dry. Every. Last. Magical. Drop.

All I had to do was touch her. *How hard could that be?*

I was about to find out.

Do it. Before it's too late. Do it now. A pulse of energy nudged me forward as I called forth my power. It accompanied the darkness egging me on, begging me to take her source. That was part of the burden of being a clàr silte. I had to fight harder than other witches to keep my magic pure, and it was nearly impossible when the power I absorbed was dark. Although, good or bad, any magic I stole, left blemishes on my soul.

The magic inside scared me, but I push aside all fears. To do what must be done, I needed to be strong and confident. The second I made the decision to take her power, my own leapt with excitement and anticipation. It roared to the surface, my eyes glowing like polished amethyst. Solely concentrating on my hands and feet, I felt the binds snap, and my body was trembling with the power that granted my freedom.

Eyes closed, the circle was oblivious that their host of power was about to break the chain. My knees and legs were a bit shaky as I pushed slowly to my feet. Amara was directly in front of me, only a few feet of space between us. Once I made contact, there was nothing she could do to stop it. I was stronger.

Careful not to even breathe, I reached out, my hand circling her wrist. "I didn't want to have to do this, Amara, but you leave me no choice."

Her eyes popped open at the sound of my voice. "There's nothing you can do to me that I can't counter." The room blanketed with darkmist, the same I'd seen in the cemetery. Nothing good ever followed the darkmist.

"That's what you think," I replied, releasing the magic humming in my veins. Thanks to the changeling spell, it was right there at the surface, ready to do my bidding. "I'm not your average witch. You should have gotten to know me before you decided to threaten my life and the life of the people I care about."

The center of her orbs went wide as she felt the first tendrils of my power weave around hers like a vine. I could see the reflection of my vibrant eyes in her glassy ones. Amara's expression was bright with fear, and I was luminous with sovereignty. Her body shuddered from the force and shock of my energy.

Everything happened faster than I expected. Either I was getting better at this, or my power was growing. Regardless, it didn't sit well in my stomach. The moment I released her, Amara fell to the ground just outside the circle. I had to wonder if any of the girls knew what they were about to do, or if they'd all been under Amara's incantation. The others glanced back and forth to each other, eyes shifting over the room, clarity beginning to break through the cloudy haze.

Except Amara. She looked like she was going to chop me up into bits and feed me to a pack of dogs. That was usually the response I got when sucking the magic from a witch. I'd expected nothing short of rage. "You bitch!" she screamed.

Gavin came flying down the stairs just as Amara lunged herself at me. "Bri!" he cried in part relief, part worry.

I didn't have time to respond, because I was sailing through the air with Amara's hands on my throat.

Oh, for the love of God...

Chapter Eleven

She didn't have any magic, whereas I was supercharged. I waited until my back hit the ground, the impact jarring my head, but I managed to keep it from smacking the ground, and then I threw my hands out.

Sparks fluttered.

Amara was suspended in the air, arms and legs spread out. She was glaring down above me, practically spitting in my face with anger. "You're the devil!" she screamed.

I angled my head. "Not quite. I'm a clàr silte. I warned you."

"Adam," she whispered, her eyes darting to the

spot where her boyfriend had been. He was nothing but charred ash. The moment I'd taken her magic, all her spells dismantled.

Gavin reached me, murmuring my name.

I sat up, wincing. My body had been hammered to the ground one too many times in a single day. His hands tenderly cupped my cheeks, sliding across my skin in the most delicious way. Moving slowly, his eyes savored my face before he pressed his lips to mine. "Don't ever do that again," he murmured.

"I don't plan on it,"

"What does a guy have to do to keep you safe?"

I shrugged, a barely-there smile on my lips. "Lock me in a tower?" I jokingly suggested.

But by the look in his dark blue eyes, he appeared to be contemplating the ridiculous notion.

"Never going to happen," I said, before he took the idea a step past only thinking. "What did she do to you?" I asked, softly running my fingers over his cheek.

His eyes glittered like diamonds as he recalled the events in the cemetery. I knew that look. He wanted to make someone pay for hurting me, but had no one on whom to unleash his anger. "Amara used a spell to knock us out."

Dark magic could often be stronger than pure

magic. Unless you were like me...a bit of both. "And you still managed to find me." I took a moment to appreciate that we were both alive, and how good it felt to be in his arms.

"Nothing would stop me finding you. Not the dead. Not a spell."

It was good to have someone who never gave up, who loved me as much as he did, who would fight until the end of time alongside me. I wanted to keep it that way. "I was so worried that she'd—"

He pressed a finger to my lip silencing me. "Don't even think it. I'm fine. We're fine."

I nodded and wrapped my arms around his neck, pressing my face against his. "She wanted to channel my power to bring back someone she lost."

"What are you going to do about her?" His eyes moved upward.

Good question. I couldn't leave her dangling in the air, however tempting. I pulled back, glancing at Amara, still floating in the air. But first, we needed to take care of her sorority sisters. They all had that WTF look on their faces. "You handle them, while I take care of her?"

We couldn't just let them go, not after what they knew about me. I wasn't a killer, so there was only one option left. We needed to wipe their memories. The deal was, though, that there was always the chance the other witches could find a way to recover the lost memories, but Amara, being only human now, would have to find another witch to regain hers. Of course, she would also have to remember a witch had taken them.

It was imperative that my identity stayed hidden, for my safety and others.

The moment he stood up and turned around, the silent room erupted into squeals and shrills as the circle broke and scrambled. Gavin cut them off at the bottom of the stairs, blocking their only escape. "Not so fast, ladies." And before anyone twitched their finger, Gavin fabricated the spell to extract memories. The swirl of green and blue mist interwove among the other girls. All it took was a whiff, and time lapsed to the exact moment before the coven had joined the circle.

They might be fuzzy and disoriented for the day, but there would no long term affects. I couldn't say the same for myself. Already, mere minutes after taking Amara's magic, I sensed the darkness she wielded, flowing through my veins.

I would be a fool not o feel some apprehension. And a fool I was not.

Understanding quickly dawned in Amara's eyes when I angled my head to look up at her. "This won't hurt; I promise," I mocked.

"Don't touch me!" she screamed.

I should have thought about sealing her mouth closed.

Her green eyes went wild as I fed the spell into the air, watching it gather around her pretty face. "You should have listened to me, but I guess like the saying goes, hindsight is twenty-twenty."

For Amara, I had a special spell. It was more than memory wiping. I was also implanting a new ending. Once I had her enthralled, all remembrance of me taking her powers gone, I carefully set her on her feet and stared in her eyes. "I'm sorry, Amara, but something went terribly wrong. The spell didn't work. Adam is gone. Forever. Do you understand?"

Big, fat tears welled in her eyes. "Gone," she sobbed. She shook her head in disbelief.

"Gone. He's in a better place now," I told her. "The spell did something to your magic. You're no longer a witch."

"What?" she gasped, her voice thick with emotion.

I know I was piling on a lot of heavy stuff, but there was no other way. "You're going to be okay. You're a strong person. You have the sorority to lean on."

She nodded, sniffing. "I do."

"They're waiting for you upstairs," I said, softening my tone.

"Why are you being so nice to me?"

Good question. I wanted to roll my eyes, but I after I thought on it, I realized it was simple. "Because I know what it's like to lose someone. I know what it's like to miss someone so much, you'd give anything to see them again. I know what it's like to feel alone."

She gave one last glance at the center of the circle, her eyes running over the chair I'd be confined to, and the place where Adam had been. Without an argument, Amara walked numbly to the stairs. In a sad way, she reminded me of the dead she raised—lost and empty.

Strong arms circled me from behind. "Think you can walk out of here, or do you need me to carry you?"

I leaned back, relaxing for the first time in what felt like weeks. Turning in his arms, I pressed my face into his chest. "I'm fine."

"Do you feel good enough for this?" he rasped, leaning down and brushing his lips across mine. The most amazing scent drifted from him. Crisp and fresh, like a walk in the woods on an autumn morning. But most of all, he smelled familiar.

I nipped the ring at his bottom lip. "As soon as

you get me out of here. This place has gone far past giving me the heebie-jeebies."

He chuckled softly.

I knew college wouldn't be easy, but *deadly* hadn't crossed my mind.

* * *

The door jingled as I walked into Madame Cora's shop. It seemed like a lifetime ago, the last time I'd been here with Tori and Austin. I felt a sense of déjà vu. Then I hadn't known what I was or what I was capable of. It was a different experience walking into the mystical shop now. I recognized the ripple of magic. I sensed the importance of the items she sold, from crystals to books—each had a purpose.

As did I.

Already, I could feel the darkmist of Amara's magic spreading on my soul. There was only one way to cure the scar left behind from taking the magic from a witch, especially a witch who practiced dark magic.

Moondust.

The End

Sign up for J.L. Press and receive a bonus scene told from Zane's POV and a free copy of Saving Angel (Book One in the bestselling Divisa Series)

http://www.jlweil.com/vip-readers

Stalk with Me Online:

Website: http://www.jlweil.com

Twitter: @JLWeil

Facebook: http://www.facebook.com/#!/jenniferlweil

About the Author

USA TODAY bestselling author J. L. Weil lives in Illinois where she writes teen & new Adult paranormal romances about spunky, smart-mouthed girls who always wind up in dire situations. For every sassy girl, there is an equally mouthwatering, overprotective guy. Of course, there is also lots of kissing. And stuff.

An admitted addict to Love Pink clothes, raspberry mochas from Starbucks, and Jensen Ackles, she loves gushing about books and *Supernatural* with her readers.

She is the author of the international bestselling Raven & Divisa series.

Read More from J. L. Weil

http://tinyurl.com/zpnhlt6

www.jlweil.com/

Made in the USA
Coppell, TX
14 May 2020

25644859R00056